longing for

langston

brody & liv

book 1
(a novella)

RENEE VINCENT

LONGING FOR LANGSTON: (BRODY & LIV)
Copyright © 2015, Renee Vincent
Digital ISBN: 978-0-99673-631-2
Trade Paperback ISBN: 978-0-99673-633-6

Cover Art Design by Renee Vincent
Stock Art by BigStock.com
Editor, Linda Ingmanson

Digital Release: November, 2015
Trade Paperback Release: November, 2015

For Olivia, Martha, and Stacey

You make the best beta readers in the world, and I thank you so much for caring about my work, my integrity, and my career. I'm a very fortunate author.

LONGING FOR LANGSTON
Mavericks of Meeteetse, Novella Book 1 (Brody & Liv)

Tired of living in his brother's shadow, Brody Galven wants the folks of Meeteetse to realize he's no longer a bad-boy screw up. He also wants his childhood best friend, Olivia Langston. While staying out of trouble proves impossible, admitting he loves her is out of the question. But will he still feel that way when she's about to walk out of his life forever?

Chapter One

Brody Galven lifted his beer to his lips and sucked it down as he stared at the woman waiting tables at the other end of the bar. He leaned back in his chair and stretched his long legs. At the same time, he took a lengthy gander at hers. His goody-two-shoes older brother, Rod, would have scolded him for doing such a thing, but thankfully, he wasn't there. Instead, he chased his less than appropriate thoughts with the rest of his beer and continued to feast his eyes on her.

The locals knew her as Olivia, but he called her Liv. She had hair like midnight and eyes like ice, a combination that everyone in this backward town thought odd and unnatural. To Brody, they were what made her beautiful, as unique and unparalleled as a perky pink flower on a prickly cactus.

Though they'd grown up together, she never ceased to amaze him. No matter what the girl did, she could do it just as well or better than anyone.

She could fish.

Hunt.

Ride.

Sing.

And kiss like nobody he'd ever kissed before.

Brody smiled, remembering that first and only kiss he'd shared with her.

It had happened one night on her twenty-third birthday. She'd been working the late shift at the Wagon Wheel and, as always, he sat in the parking lot on the tailgate of his truck waiting for her to get off work, so he could give her a lift home. When he heard the bar door burst open and his name squeal from her lips, he spun around just in time to catch her leaping into his arms. His cowboy hat hit the ground, and his heart soared. She'd finally landed an agent for her singing career, and before he could really understand what that meant, she planted a kiss on his lips.

At first, it was just a quick peck, an innocent gesture punctuating her excitement for something she'd tried for years to score. But as soon as she realized what she'd done, her smile faded.

Brody remembered how rigid Olivia's body felt against his as they held each other's gaze. The last thing he wanted was for her to push away and apologize. So, he bent and kissed her back. Only this time, it was slow and easy. Nothing felt more right than tasting her lips and feeling her body sink into his chest.

As he sat there, remembering how soft and warm her mouth felt on his, he also recalled the look in her eyes. He swore he saw a glimmer of unrestrained lust in them. As if at any moment, she'd tear his clothes off and have her way with him.

But what did he know?

A few seconds after he'd cupped her face and deepened the kiss, she pulled back and stared at him as if he had three heads.

To save face, he had played it off like no big deal and broke away from her with as much aloofness as he could fake. He swiped his hat from the ground and made some excuse about having to get her home right away so she could tell her mama the good news. Little did she know he was just trying to lessen the amount of time he had left to spend with her in case she was itching to discuss the matter exhaustively.

In hindsight, Brody was damn glad she hadn't called him out for crossing the line. He broke the friend code by following directions from something far more demanding than his brain. Most guys would've caught a slap across the face or a knee to the nether region for what he had pulled. Lucky for him, his Liv wasn't that kind of girl. *Just roll with it* was her usual motto.

Since then, Liv had never brought it up and he had

never tried anything like that again. But it didn't mean his hormones quit raging. To the best of his ability, he resorted to admire her from afar and do his damnedest to keep it off the radar. Some days that was easier said than done—like tonight.

Though Liv had grown up a tomboy, Brody couldn't help but notice the feminine curves she crammed into her cutoff denim shorts. Hell, even the knot she tied in her shirt just below her breasts tempted him to pull it free.

Get a grip, Brody. She's off-limits and you know it.

He fidgeted in his seat, growing uncomfortable in his own tight denim jeans. Olivia Langston might be his best friend—heck, his only friend—but she drove him absolutely wild.

Brody adjusted his hat and leaned forward, resting both elbows on the table. He regarded the flirtatious smile she offered to a group of guys who'd ordered a round, and decided it didn't sit well with him.

She'd argue it was just for tips.

He'd argue it was too much.

That was the meat and potatoes of their relationship. If she wasn't doing something to either turn him on or tick him off, she was getting herself in a situation where he had to step in and save her.

From where he sat, he sized up all three of the

newcomers, determining whether he'd need help if a fight broke out. Unfortunately, the folks in this establishment mostly resembled those from a retirement home rather than a cowboy bar. He'd be on his own this time.

Liv glanced his way as if she felt the weight of his gaze bearing down on her. To downplay the fact that he'd been caught staring, he picked up his empty beer bottle and shook it, signaling he needed another. She nodded once and dismissed him, only to offer another pretty smile to the three dudes in the booth.

Brody crossed his arms and growled under his breath. At times, he hated her job. Especially when she had to act all sweet and kind to a bunch of cheesy-smiling, smooth-talking city slickers who thought they were genuine cowboys because they wore a hat and boots. Brody took one glance at the shiny black leather gleaming from their Tony Lamas. They were no more acquainted with the dust and manure of a cattle ranch than he was acquainted with driving a Bentley.

A sudden surge of male laughter resounded from their corner, and Brody caught sight of a well-manicured hand reaching out and touching Liv's elbow. The man did his best to pour on the charm before his hand fell away and brushed her leg on the way down.

Brody tensed, ready to step in and crush every single

one of those highfalutin fingers in his fist, but Liv would be furious with him. His chest burned as he tried to curb his temper for her sake. He bounced his leg on the ball of his foot, just itching to bolt out of his chair and teach this ill-bred urban cowboy a lesson in manners.

Liv stepped politely out of the man's reach and waited on the wannabe cowboy across from him. This guy seemed less forward than his friend, but no less fake. As he made some tasteless comment about Liv choosing the heat level on his wings, the third chump glanced up from his menu and spotted Brody glowering. He turned white and swallowed, elbowing his buddy. A few words passed between them before they all, including Liv, peered down the length of the barroom to where Brody sat.

He didn't have to stand to reveal his massive six-foot-three frame. He assumed he looked menacing enough as he stewed in his seat. His colorful sleeve of tatts on both forearms lent their share of intimidation as well.

Brody dared them to do anything—say anything—that was the least bit out of line. To his disappointment, all three shrank behind the wall of the booth and wrapped up their order with Liv.

She faked a smile in front of her customers and made some excuse that he was harmless, before she threw Brody a look and withdrew to the kitchen.

He didn't take kindly to the notion that she considered him harmless. When it came to her, he was about as harmless as a stalled stallion in a barn full of mares.

Minutes later, Liv rounded the bar with a bucket of beer and set it in the middle of the newcomers' table with another pleasant smile. She gave them some practiced spiel about her name should they need anything else before she patted one of them on the shoulder.

Brody rolled his eyes in time to see her marching his way. She stopped short of his table and slammed a beer in front of him. "Do you mind? I'm trying to work here, Galven."

Brody eyed the white foam racing to the top of the bottle, bubbling over the lip. He hated a beer full of head. "I'm going to need another one of these."

She lunged forward, planting both hands on the table. "I'm serious, Brody. Knock off the badass-boyfriend routine, will ya? I need their tips, and I'm not going to get anything with you giving them the evil eye."

Brody gazed into Olivia's gorgeous eyes. The temptation to look down her shirt killed him, but he never wavered. He had more respect for her than that, which was more than he could say for most of the customers who bellied up to this bar. Not to mention the trio of tenderfoots she had waited on.

"Are you listening to me?" she asked, stomping her foot.

Brody didn't mean to smile. It just happened.

Liv grumbled and snatched his frothy beer to exchange it. "I'm never going to get to Nashville at this rate."

Brody caught her hand, stopping her in her tracks. He liked the feel of it in his. To be truthful, he wished he could twirl her into his arms, tip her back, and kiss the daylights out of her.

She planted her free hand on her hip. "What now, Galven?"

The words she'd muttered echoed in his ears. *"I'm never going to get to Nashville at this rate."*

If anyone knew how badly she wanted to start her singing career in Nashville, it was Brody. For years, she'd dreamt of making it big and living off her voice instead of tips from yuppie city folk passing through on their vacation. After she landed that agent, everyone thought, including Brody, it was only a matter of time before she gained a big record deal.

That was last year, and still...she hadn't heard anything.

Brody softened his grip and patted the top of her wrist. "I'm sorry, Liv. I know how much that dream means to you." He peeled her fingers from the bottle and took a swig, enduring the watery taste of the flat beer. "I'll leave right after I finish this...skunk piss."

"Give me that," she said, smiling. "And you don't have to leave. It's fine."

He glanced around her at the three fellas in the distant booth. "You sure?"

"Yes, I'm sure. But chill out, okay? I can take care of myself."

"Yeah, well, I don't want anyone to take advantage of you. Men are pigs."

Liv's soft laughter immediately brightened his mood. "Are you including yourself in that statement?"

He thought about the many times he'd sweet-talked his way into a girl's heart. He could admit he was a giant pig with girls he didn't care about. But Liv was different. She deserved respect and a man who'd treat her right. Which was why he occasionally took out his sexual frustrations on girls who hadn't a care for their own self-respect.

"All men are pigs, Liv."

She blew out a dry laugh this time and shook her head. "I'll be back with your beer in a sec."

Brody watched her walk away, his gaze automatically falling to her tight little butt. He couldn't help but be mesmerized by its subtle sway, which had him wishing he and Liv weren't friends at all.

Yep. We men are pigs.

"Here you go," Liv said, handing him a fresh beer. He nearly jumped at the sound of her voice, unaware that he'd been carried off by his perverse sexual thoughts.

"Uh...thanks."

"You all right there, Galven?" She removed his Stetson and straightened his hair before plopping it back on his head. "Long day at the McKinley ranch?"

Brody cleared his throat, thankful she couldn't read his mind. He reached up and readjusted his hat the way he preferred it. Only Liv could get away with touching it. "Yeah, you could say that."

"Well, you sit back and enjoy your beer. I gotta sing in a few."

Liv dragged her fingertips along his arm and over his shoulder as she headed toward the stage in the back of the bar. He closed his eyes, relishing the feel of her touch for a few seconds while he tried to collect himself. As innocent as it might have been, that little brush of hers caused a whole cataclysm of sensations to run through his body. His groin tightened. His blood coursed through his veins. And his heart ached so deep in his chest, he thought it might burst.

He didn't know how much longer he could go through life just being her friend. He desired Liv more than anything, but it was too risky to tell her how he truly felt. Things would get awkward if he started sleeping with her. They always did when friends tried the benefits thing.

And what if she didn't feel the same in return? What if she didn't want to share that kind of intimacy with him? Or worse…maybe she *did*. And because she loved him so darn much, she'd turn down her chance to go to Nashville when the call came.

Brody's lids shot open the moment he heard the strum of her guitar and the sweet angelic tenor of her voice in the microphone behind him. Chills ran over his body every time she opened her beautiful mouth to sing.

Yeah…she'd be better off never knowing how he felt. She deserved to make it big and be happy. Besides, he knew one day she *would* get that call. And it'd be that much harder for him to say good-bye if he were sleeping with her.

Chapter Two

Taking a deep breath, Brody turned his chair around and faced the stage. He put on his happy face for Liv and drowned his aching heart with the rest of his cold beer. For the next few blessed minutes, he leaned back and enjoyed the acoustic one-woman show of Liv Langston, the only worthwhile entertainment offered at the Wagon Wheel— every hour on the hour.

He scanned the room as she hit and held a high note. About ten people, all of them regulars save for the corner booth of fancy Nancies, had gathered to mingle and be merry. Some came to eat. Some came to drink a few with friends. And some sat in quiet retrospection, smoking their choice of tobacco. But as of right now, every eye was glued to the dark-haired beauty in cutoffs. She rolled into the familiar bridge of an old Patsy Cline number, then segued into a classic George Jones song. He sat proud, watching her strum that beat-up six-string and listening to her rekindle new life into so many great vintage tunes.

As she brought her set to an end, a roar of cheers and applause erupted. Even a few piercing whistles split the joy and excitement of the meager crowd. Brody clapped as he watched Liv smile and bow in humble gratitude. It wouldn't be long before she'd be singing in front of thousands of fans. He just knew it.

Liv hung her guitar on the wall behind her and stepped off the platform to resume her waitress duties. Brody caught her attention and pointed to his empty bottle. *One more*, he mouthed.

She gave him the thumbs-up and walked between tables, checking on customers and snagging empties as she went. Just like that, the atmosphere of the Wagon Wheel returned to its usual state. The local drunkard, Bob Walsh, plopped his forehead on his arm and took another snooze on the slick lacquered wood of the bar. Mr. Corinth sat beside him, puffing on his cigar and watching Denver kick Cleveland into the dirt. His wife ignored the game and the few Bronco fans who sat adjacent to her. Instead, she perched on her stool, crocheting the beginnings of a tricolored afghan. On the opposite end near the restrooms, Professor Shoemaucker hid behind his newspaper as he always did on Monday evenings.

Everything was as it should be, save for the three guys in the corner booth. Brody kept refocusing his attention on them, waiting for one of the spoiled pretty boys to act out of line. He knew they would. He'd bet money on it. Especially the guy with the million-dollar smile and the thousand-dollar wristwatch. He had more flash than a vintage mid-century Kodak camera. Guys like that loved to be the center of attention and often went to extremes to acquire it.

"You're doing it again, Galven," Liv interrupted, handing Brody a full one.

"Doing what?"

"Sizing them up. Finding justification for kicking their asses." Liv seized his chin and drew his attention toward her. "Let it go. I mean it."

Though she stood no taller than five foot four, weighing in at a buck ten, Brody adored her confidence. She embodied self-assurance in the way she turned and sashayed down the aisle of empty tables. He held his beer to his lips as he watched her drop another bucket of beers at the corner booth. Her long, toned legs flexed as she leaned forward. Her shorts barely covered that spot where the curve of her bottom met the back of her thigh. If he wasn't so suspicious of the guys at that table, he might have bought them another round just so he could watch Liv stretch and lean again.

"Well, thank you, darlin'," Brody heard one say.

"That's mighty kind of you."

For a moment, Brody thought perhaps he'd judged them prematurely. It wouldn't have been the first time he'd allowed his jealous tendencies to bring out the worst in him. The last time it happened, he'd ended up spending the night in jail for disorderly conduct. He'd never forget that awful night. He only wished the folks of Meeteetse would.

No sooner had Brody given those boys the benefit of the doubt than one of them reached around and slapped her on the behind. When she scowled at him, the man laughed and pulled her onto his lap.

Liv shrieked in surprise and writhed to escape him. Brody flipped his lid and lunged from his chair without hesitation. He gritted his teeth. Spots blurred his vision. He was going to kill that sonofabitch.

Liv saw Brody stalking forward. She froze. She looked more frightened than the two guys who tried to warn their friend. Upping the effort, she threw an elbow into the man's chest and slipped from his grasp. "Galven, wait!" she said, throwing herself at Brody. "Listen to me. He isn't worth it." She frantically pointed toward the bar behind him. "See, Jethro's coming. He'll throw them out, and they won't be allowed back. Please, Brody, listen to me. Don't do this."

Brody could hear Liv pleading, but nothing registered.

He moved her aside and barreled forward. All three guys had squeezed out of the booth, securing their spot in a defensive triangle. The biggest of the three stood in the front.

Brody scoffed, unimpressed with any of them. "I don't know where you're from, but around here, we treat women with respect."

The entire bar fell silent. No one dared to move a muscle with Brody cocked and loaded.

"You don't want to mess with me," the stranger stated, crossing his arms. "I'll have you know my father is the—"

"I don't care who your sperm donor is," Brody interrupted. "Apologize to her."

Brody felt Liv's hand on his shoulder. "It—it's okay."

"No, it isn't." Brody stared the man down. "Apologize. Now."

One of the three muttered to the guy in front, "Apologize already so we can get the hell out of here, Carlton."

"Your friend's a smart man," Brody added. "You should listen to him."

Carlton shook his head. "I don't have to listen to you or anybody in this Podunk town. And I sure as hell don't need to apologize to a *waitress*. It's her job to serve me. Besides, I think she liked having a *real* man's arms around her for a change." He leaned forward and looked Brody in the eyes. "What do you think about that? *Hillbilly.*"

Brody reared back and threw the first punch, knocking Carlton and his high-dollar hat into next Sunday. His two friends caught and steadied him, aghast at the blood spewing from Carlton's nose. Carlton shook the dizziness from his brain and sprang forward only to find himself in Brody's clutches again. From there, Brody tossed him headfirst across the table, knocking beer bottles and aluminum buckets on the floor. Glass shattered at his feet as he took hold of Carlton's shirt collar and lifted him upright for another go-round.

A horrendous commotion filled the bar as every able man jumped in to pull them apart.

"Hey, hey, hey, bro! That's enough!"

Brody heard Rod's voice amid all the chaos and felt a multitude of hands clutching his shoulders and arms. He looked in the eyes of his older brother and huffed like a freight train.

Clouded by rage, he had a difficult time understanding how Rod had come to be there in the first place. He glared at his brother, then at the many hands upon him.

"Calm down, brother," Rod said, righting Brody's hat, which had shifted off-center. He gave his left cheek a brotherly pat. "You're good. You got this."

Brody shook everyone off and shoved Rod backward. "Get off me!"

Rod stepped forward and didn't back down. "Enough. You're scaring the good people of Meeteetse here. Settle down. Take a breath. Get your bearings. It's over."

Brody drew in a long, steady breath and blew it out, glowering at Rod for getting involved. This wasn't his fight, nor did he have a clue what had gone on.

"Stay out of this, Rod."

"I can't do that, and you know it. You're my brother, and I'm not going to let you do something you'll regret later."

"Regret?" Brody almost laughed. "The only thing I regret is that I didn't throw this lowlife out the minute he sat down."

"Actually, it's not your decision who stays or goes, Brody. That would be my say."

Slowly and very meticulously, Brody turned his head until he found Jethro. He knew even before he laid eyes on him that the bar owner had made the comment. He was the one who had pressed charges against Brody years ago for a fight he didn't start. "Are you taking up for this asshole too? Did you not see what he did to Ms. Langston?"

Jethro splayed his hands in front of him and swallowed hard. "All I know is, I got one hell of a mess to clean up because you decided to take matters into your own hands. Again."

"Yeah, well, I didn't see you doing anything to help her. Is that how you treat your female employees? Turn a blind eye to gross sexual assault?"

To everyone's surprise, Carlton finally spoke up in his defense as he swiped his bloody nose across his sleeve. "Hey, hey, look, I didn't sexually assault anyone. All I did was have a little fun. Right, doll?"

Brody swiveled around and pointed at Carlton over Rod's shoulder. "You shut your mouth!"

"Brody, cool it," Rod cautioned.

"Not until he apologizes to Liv."

"Like I said," Carlton piped up again, making sure there was enough blood on his sleeve for evidence. "I'm not apologizing to anyone. Unless you want to defend your own assault charge, Hillbilly, you might want to apologize to *me*."

"Why, you no good, motherfu—"

This time, Rod had to use all his strength to hold Brody back. Carlton staggered backward, clearly fearing for his life. Jethro stepped in, probably fearing a lawsuit. "Rod, get your brother out of here before he gets me sued."

Chapter Three

Brody stumbled out the door and into the parking lot with his brother on his heels. Rod shoved him with each step, ushering him farther from the bar until they reached Brody's vehicle.

"You want to explain what the hell happened in there?"

Brody leaned his forearms on the bed of his truck and caught his breath. He couldn't blame his brother for throwing him out of the Wagon Wheel. He knew Rod only wanted what was best for him and didn't want to see him in trouble with the law again.

On the flip side, he was mad as hell at him for it. Rod had made a complete fool out of him in front of everyone, not to mention that city slicker, Carlton. He recalled those in the bar who remembered his days of being a nuisance teen and how disappointed they looked at him now. He hated that the folks of Meeteetse still saw him that way, but he was only trying to do what was right. Surely, they'd agree that no woman should be treated that way. Maybe they hadn't seen what happened to her. Maybe they thought he was trying to start trouble again.

"Well?" Rod asked, smacking Brody upside the head.

Brody caught Rod's wrist and threw his brother's hand back at him. "I was trying to get the guy to apologize to Liv. He refused. He mouthed off. I got mad."

"Yeah, yeah, yeah. Same old story, Brody. When are you going to learn that you can't fix everything with your fists?"

"You saw him, Rod. There's no talking to guys like him."

"And there's no talking to guys like you either. All you want to do is pound someone in the ground. Over what? A girl you've got the hots for but don't have the guts to tell her?"

Brody quickly scanned the parking lot and the front porch of the bar for Liv, hoping she wasn't around to hear their conversation. "Will you shut your mouth, Rod? She can't know how I feel."

"Why? Why won't you tell her? I don't get it."

"It's not for you to understand. It's how I feel. It's my prerogative. Not yours."

Rod removed his cowboy hat and ran his hand through his hair, pacing between the vehicles. "That may be so, Brody, but you've got to pull it together. If you don't have the nerve to make a move on Olivia, then you can't get mad at every dude who does."

"The douchebag slapped her on the ass and practically shoved his hand between her legs, Rod!"

"Every red-blooded male in Meeteetse wants to. Including you."

Brody launched himself at Rod, grabbing his brother by the shirt. "Don't talk like that about Liv."

Rod chuckled in Brody's face. "See? There you go again. Defending her as if she's yours. Protecting her like you're her knight in shining armor." Rod broke away from his brother's hold and poked Brody's chest. "What are you going to do when she falls in love with someone one day? Hmm? What are you going to do when that someone isn't *you*? You going to kick his ass? Bloody his nose? Go to jail—again? 'Cause that's what's going to happen. One of these days you're going to wind up back in jail because of your temper. And this time it'll be because you messed with the wrong guy." Rod pointed toward the bar. "Like that guy in there who has connections. Who has weight behind his daddy's name, who can get charges to stick. Is that what you want?"

"No. But I'd do it. For her."

Rod scoffed. "You'd do time for her?"

Brody smirked at his brother, knowing he was only trying to get to him. "I'm not afraid, if that's what you're asking."

"You're not afraid because there's always been someone to bail you out. Always been someone in Meeteetse who knows and pities Mama for the hell she's been through since Daddy died. Always been someone who'll come to your rescue because they're hoping maybe this time you'll change."

Brody looked out at the distant Absaroka Mountains. The wide, majestic, snow-capped range reminded him of the times he and his father went fishing in the Greybull River. A time when he remembered being happy. A time when there wasn't such a thing as a huge chasm within his family.

Since his father's passing, Rod had stepped in to fill the void and take care of things as the man of the household, including watching out for Brody. He knew Rod made it his responsibility to keep him on the straight and narrow.

"You don't have to watch out for me anymore. I'm a grown man."

"Well, I've got news for you, Brody. One of these days, I'm not going to be around to save you. Or maybe one day…I just decide you're not worth saving."

Rod could've hacked him with a chainsaw and it

would've hurt less. The wound his hurtful words left behind gaped open and left him to stand there weak and speechless.

Olivia called Brody's name, and, until that moment, he'd had no idea she had stepped outside. Her pace quickened once she located him in the gravel lot with Rod. Her face was full of concern and questions that he wasn't ready to address.

He drew in a much-needed breath and cleared his foggy brain. He needed to get away. To be alone with his thoughts. To distance himself from the righteous brother who cast a shadow too large for Brody to be seen.

Without so much as a good-bye, Brody ducked around his truck and climbed inside. Unable to face Liv, he turned the key. From his peripheral vision, she laid her palms on his passenger-side window and rapped on it.

"Where are you going?"

Without even glancing her way, Brody knew there was panic in her eyes as she looked to his brother for answers.

"Rod, where's Brody going?"

Rod pulled her out of harm's way as Brody revved the engine. "He's all right. He just needs some space."

Brody's jaw hurt from grinding his teeth so hard. He threw the shifter into drive and pulled out, leaving a wake of dust behind him.

****

Olivia stormed back inside the bar, and a wall of curious faces met her, none of which she acknowledged. The only person she did talk to was Jethro, her boss. She watched him sweep up the last of the glass around the corner booth before divulging her plans.

"I have to leave."

Jethro's eyes widened in surprise. "You can't leave. You're still on the clock."

"Then I'm taking myself off. Besides, you kicked my ride home out of the bar, remember? Now all I have is Rod." She glanced at the clock on the wall. "You have an hour and a half before closing. Surely, you can fill a few drink orders."

On a mission, she turned to collect her purse from the kitchen and almost ran into the three strangers coming out of the restroom. She stopped mid-stride, uncertain what to say. Her moral upbringing reminded her to say *Excuse me*, while her impulsive resentful side wanted to impart a good old-fashioned *F you*.

Carlton had obviously cleaned himself up, save for the bright red bloodstain on the sleeve of his white shirt. His cowboy hat, once pressed with clean, smooth, symmetrical ridges, had dents and arcs in random places, making it appear lopsided on his head.

Olivia bit back a smile and circled them without saying a word. When she waltzed back into the dining area, she couldn't help but notice that Carlton and his friends had found a seat at a different booth, with another round of beers, only this time they were in cold, frosty mugs. Probably on the house.

Liv seethed. She wasn't sure who she should be angrier with, Jethro for allowing them to stay, or the guys who thought they were welcome to after the ruckus they'd caused.

Rod stepped inside the bar and must have noticed the same thing. Olivia saw his forehead furrow a bit over the whole scene and wondered if he were going to call attention to it. He had as much muscle as Brody to back up his dissatisfaction and a lot more clout with the folks of this small town. If anyone could get these guys thrown out without much dispute, it was Rod. To her disappointment, he shrugged it off.

"You ready?" he murmured, crossing his arms.

She was ready, all right. Ready to make a stand. She had no idea where she'd gotten her sudden shot of fearlessness, but it hit her like a bolt of lightning. "One second, Rod." She slapped her purse against his chest and stomped toward their booth.

A sweet, bright smile split Olivia's lips as she regarded their uneasy glances. "You boys need anything else before I leave?"

Carlton smiled and set down his beer. He cleared his throat and, like the snake he was, slithered into that fake charming demeanor he'd used moments before he got his ass handed to him. "I don't believe we do, darlin'." He surveyed her up and down as if she were on the menu.

Olivia kept her cool and charmed him right back. "Wonderful. Then have a great evening." With that, she reached across the table and grabbed all three mugs by their handles, busing in one fell swoop.

"Hey, hey, hey there. What do you think you're doing?"

"I'm sorry," Olivia simpered, glancing at the three full beer mugs in her possession and back at Carlton. "Did you still want these?"

Carlton smirked at her as if she were an idiot. "Well, yeah…" He had the earmarks of a genuine know-it-all as he remarked behind the shield of his hand, "They don't make 'em too bright up here, do they?"

Olivia flashed the biggest self-satisfied smile and poured all three mugs into Carlton's lap. Carlton jumped up, his crotch soaking wet. "What the hell? You just poured beer all over me!"

"Wow, look who the bright one is now," Olivia jeered. She saw Rod finally making his way toward the booth. "You think this guy's smart enough to know when he's outworn his welcome?"

Carlton backed up, putting some space between him and Rod. He searched the bar, hoping he'd snag just a notion of pity from someone—anyone. But every individual in the Wagon Wheel stared at him with stoic, unsympathetic eyes. Even Jethro seemed reluctant to jump on his bandwagon.

Mrs. Corinth, with her crochet needle and yarn, slipped off her barstool and stepped forward, aligning herself with Olivia. "Young man, I think it's time for you and your friends to go home. Rod? Will you kindly finish what your brother started and show these gentlemen to the door?"

"My pleasure, ma'am." Rod straightened his hat and angled his body toward the door, extending his hand. "This way, boys."

Carlton and his friends wasted no time leaving. Like reprimanded puppies, they scurried out the door and shuffled across the parking lot to their tinted-windowed, white diamond Escalade.

Olivia watched out the window until the luxury utility vehicle pulled onto the road before hugging Mrs. Corinth.

She thanked the seventy-year-old woman for speaking up, wishing the rest of the people in the bar would've done the same for Brody. He was the one who deserved the support.

As she snatched her purse from Rod's hand, she smacked his arm with it. "You owe your brother an apology. You know that, right?"

Rod shook his head as he held the door open for her. "I guess I'm going to find out all about why on the way, ain't I?"

"And then some."

Chapter Four

Olivia opened the door to Rod's Chevy pickup and looked at him from the passenger seat. "Are you sure Brody's here?"

"I know my brother. Whenever he's mad, this is where he comes to blow off a little steam. Trust me."

"I know this is where he normally hides out, Rod. This ain't my first rodeo. But I don't see his truck."

"Check the woodshed." He pointed out his window toward the other side of the barn.

Olivia nodded and thanked him for the lift, hopping out of his vehicle. The sound of gravel crunched under her boots, cutting the quiet stillness of the evening. With the time being close to nine-thirty, she felt uneasy wandering around the McKinley ranch in the dark. She hoped she wouldn't end up disturbing them.

Jonas McKinley, a third generation farmer, was a handsome thirty-something-year-old who'd owned the ranch since his father died about ten years ago. His girlfriend, Ava Wallace, lived with him in the single-story log cabin, and they ran the farm together. From the talk of the town, Olivia often heard they made a decent living. Jonas and his friend, Cole Forester, took care of the cattle end of the business, while Ava managed the public trail riding tours. Each had their own set of employees to help with the daily chores. Rod and Brody were Jonas's workers, but every now and again, Brody would talk about how he'd have to step in as a trail guide for Ava when one of her girls called in sick.

Brody was the jack-of-all-trades kind of guy, able to do just about anything. Rod, on the other hand, didn't like to stray from the usual tasks. Olivia assumed it had a lot to do with the fact that Rod was the eldest. His seniority had given him the opportunity to decline the duties he didn't care for, which forced Brody to take them on instead.

Not having to fight for control was one thing Oliva liked about being an only child. And Brody's indifference was probably what had drawn her to him in the first place. He was easier to get along with than his bossy older brother and, though Rod would argue otherwise, Brody was less dramatic. Sometimes Olivia felt that if it weren't for Rod stepping in, Brody wouldn't have to prove himself all the time.

Olivia watched as Rod drove down the long gravel lane

and inwardly cursed him for not sticking around to help her find his brother. Though she'd said her piece to him on the way there, Rod didn't seem to agree with her. He told her he knew his brother better than anyone and that Brody had a lot of growing up to do. He even went so far as to state that her perpetual support of Brody only encouraged his immature behavior and that he'd never learn to be a real man if she continued to coddle him.

As the red glow of taillights faded into the night, she flipped Rod the bird. No matter what Rod said, Brody was the more chivalrous brother in her eyes.

She rubbed her arms, feeling the chill of the night. Goose bumps spread like a California wildfire across her bare skin, and she wished she'd worn jeans to work instead of shorts.

She glanced up. Nearly full, the moon hung high in the sky, a silent watchman over the peaceful valley below. Only the moon and God knew how she truly felt about Brody, and she reckoned it would stay that way. Brody never gave her the impression he wanted more than her friendship. They'd grown so close through the years that now she figured she was more like a sister to him. He never said as much, but she knew. Call it woman's intuition.

Olivia exhaled, blowing out her frustrations, and regarded the many buildings that surrounded her. She'd been to the McKinley ranch before, but never in the dark.

To the northeast, at the base of a bluff, sat Jonas's log home with a wraparound porch. Soft, warm light from the front window illuminated the backs of two rocking chairs and a small table. Olivia imagined Jonas and Ava spending quiet evenings on the porch, sipping ice tea and listening to the crickets and frogs. She then contemplated that it might have been the very reason she hardly ever saw them at the Wagon Wheel. If she had a porch like that, she probably wouldn't venture out much either.

Across from the house was a dry lot, which then fed into a maze of pastures at the base of the Absaroka Mountains. According to Brody, Jonas McKinley owned some of the most beautiful acreage in the Bighorn Basin, encompassed by miles of blackboard fence.

Next to the dry lot stood a huge barn, a covered manure pit, a rock smokehouse, and a wood building with tiny fissures of light shining through each of the vertical slats. She assumed it to be the woodshed Rod had indicated, but in the dark, everything looked indistinguishable. The only thing that wasn't ambiguous was the smell of manure, hay, and dirt.

Though a little nervous to do so, Olivia proceeded forward. Dark shadows draped every recess and corner. Not a single light illuminated the grounds around the buildings, save for the moon. Taking a shot in the dark, she whispered Brody's name.

An outbreak of nickers and snorts erupted from inside the barn. Olivia bit her lip and swiveled her gaze toward the McKinley house, fearing Jonas might wander out with his gun.

"Is that you, Liv?"

Olivia yelped, whirling from the voice behind her. From out of the shadows, she saw Brody holding a hatchet. "Sonofabitch, Galven! You nearly gave me a heart attack." She pressed her hand to her heart and gasped for breath.

"What are you doing here?" he asked.

"What the hell are you doing with an ax?"

"Splitting wood."

"At this hour? Are you crazy?"

"There's light in the shed. And you still haven't answered *my* question."

"I came to see you." She struggled with how to explain herself without making it sound as if she were checking up on him. "To see if you needed any company."

He peered beyond her toward the driveway. "And I reckon Rod dropped you off?"

She walked toward him, hoping to see his facial expressions more clearly before she answered. "I asked him to."

Brody's head fell back, and he inhaled deeply. He looked irritated. "Aren't you supposed to be working?"

"I clocked out. And most everyone was fixing to leave anyway."

"And Jethro was okay with that?"

"What's he going to do? Fire me?" She tried to get Brody to laugh. He didn't. Instead, he crossed his arms.

"He very well could fire you."

Olivia scoffed. "He'd have to grow a set first."

This time Brody harrumphed. At least she was able to pull something from him. Past experience reminded her it wasn't going to be easy to connect with Brody. Getting him to open up would be like prying a walnut from its shell. Determined to try, she sidled up to him and reached for his hand.

He stepped away. "Look, I'm not sure why you came here tonight, Liv, but I don't really feel like talking."

Unsure what to do with her outstretched hand, Olivia tucked it under her pit and crossed her arms. "Okay. So, don't talk. I'll just watch you split wood. Besides, you're kind of my ride home now."

Brody glanced down the gravel drive and grimaced. "Right."

He sighed and walked back into the shadows between the buildings. Liv followed him, tripping on high grass and anything else she couldn't see. The strong scent of dung smacked her in the face as she passed the manure pit and turned the corner. His truck came into view first, parked perpendicular to the woodshed with the tailgate down. On it sat a cooler and two empty bottles of beer.

The shed was a three-sided building with an open front and a lean-to porch extending from the roof. In this way, wood could be split, loaded up, hauled out, or stacked inside while out of the elements.

With plenty of room to move, Brody stepped over a haphazard heap of split wood on the ground and reached inside the cooler on his tailgate. "You want one?"

Olivia joined him and leaned against his truck. She glanced at the ax he placed on the bed and frowned inwardly. "Sure."

He twisted off the top and handed it to her before resuming his work. She took a sip, observing him as he grabbed armfuls of wood and added them to a large stack against the back wall. It worried her that he'd wielded a sharp blade under the influence of alcohol. Stupid, really.

Given Brody's current state of mind, she figured she'd board that train from a different station. "So, Jonas is okay with you coming to his ranch and hanging out?"

"Why would he care?"

"I don't know." Olivia shrugged. "Because it's late.

And you're on his property. Isn't that a legal risk for him if something happened?"

Brody gauged her question as he lugged another armload. "I'd never sue Jonas. He's the only one in this town who doesn't look at me like I'm some worthless convict."

She felt the tender eggshells cracking beneath her feet. "Sure, but Jonas doesn't know if you're a sue-happy kinda guy. Nor could he guarantee—"

"Liv," Brody cut her off, his hands on his hips now. "I know what you're thinking, but for your information, I didn't drink a single beer while I split wood. And the two you see empty are from when I saw Rod pull up. I tossed them back thinking I was about to get another ass chewing. So there. Happy now?"

"Not really."

"Well, then, I don't know what to tell you. I can't fix everything for you, Liv."

Chapter Five

Brody didn't mean to lash out. When it came to Liv, he normally watched his mouth and minded his manners. Tonight, he didn't have much control over his behavior. He sighed and hung his head. "I'm sorry."

He blamed it on his brother. Rod had stuck his nose in where it didn't belong, and Rod sure as hell hadn't done him any favors by breaking up the fight. It would've been different if Rod had kicked the guys out right after he and Carlton were separated. At least it would've conveyed the notion that Rod had his back. Instead, Rod made him look like a complete fool.

Brody closed his eyes, feeling his blood begin to boil again. Splitting wood had always helped him take the edge off, but what he wouldn't give for a good old-fashioned punching bag right now.

Liv put down her beer and came to him. She stroked his forearm, trying to ease his tension. She knew him well. So much so that she monitored his clenched fists—fists he hadn't even realized he'd made until now.

He felt her fingers stroke the inside of his wrist before she clasped her hand around his. She lifted his right one and inspected the cut on his knuckle. "You don't have to apologize, Galven. I know exactly why you're mad. I'd be mad too." She ran her finger along the swelling of the laceration. "Is this from the fight?"

He loved her touch. The cool sensation of her fingertips on his hot skin whittled away his resolve. "Mm-hmm."

"I never thanked you for coming to my rescue."

He'd do it again if he had to. "You don't have to thank me." His voice came out strained and hoarse.

"I know you don't need my gratitude, but you deserve it."

She bent and placed a kiss upon his busted knuckle. He clenched his jaw to trap a groan. The feel of her lips brushing his skin damn near socked him in the gut. He'd taken hard blows in the stomach many times before, but nothing compared to this.

His brain automatically painted a picture of Liv's soft lips leaving a trail of kisses up his arm, across his collarbone, and up his neck until she reached his mouth. He envisioned her lips on his and her hands in his hair, pulling him into a deeper, passionate kiss.

On weak legs, he stepped back and bumped into the wall behind him.

Liv gawked at him, confused by his sudden need to flee. Her perplexity then turned to despair. "Does the thought of me gross you out that much, Galven?"

She waited for an answer, but he couldn't provide one. Nothing could've been further from the truth.

When he didn't reply, frustration scrunched her face and she heaved a sigh. "I'll just call Rod."

She turned and headed out of the woodshed. Brody leapt forward and caught her wrist. "Liv, wait."

He spun her around and studied the hurt in her eyes. To the average Joe, there was no evidence of pain, not even a single tear. But he knew better. The sting of rejection was there. "It's not that you gross me out."

Her brow cocked upward as she stared at her feet. He sensed her doubt.

"I was surprised, is all. You kind of caught me off guard."

She couldn't seem to look him in the eye. Why did he have to hurt her?

"Liv, please."

Her gaze slowly found his. He couldn't read her. Maybe she *did* want him the way he wanted her. Perhaps she had found the courage to let him know how she felt by initiating a heartfelt, uncomplicated kiss and he had to go and shoot her down. Or maybe he was hooked so deep on a wish that he blew every little thing she did out of proportion.

"Galven?"

He swallowed hard, trying to stay strong. He had to. For her sake. He couldn't give her a reason to hang back in Meeteetse if the call from Nashville came. Regardless of how bad she wanted it, Liv would put her dreams on hold for those she cared about, and he'd never forgive himself if he became that person.

As hard as he tried, the idea of coming clean tempted him. He could think of nothing else but blurting it out and letting the chips fall where they may. He wanted her to know exactly how he felt, to prove it with a long, hot, passionate kiss.

He could see himself picking her up in his arms and laying her down in the back seat of his truck. The sound of his name on her lips would quake the ground harder than any rumble of thunder.

Only she could truly relieve this awful pain in his heart.

"Liv, I... I need to tell you... I mean... I want..."

"Yes?" she encouraged.

Her tantalizing bottom lip distracted him. He tried again. "I want you." As soon as it rolled off his tongue, he regretted it. He sounded selfish and stupid. He couldn't do this to her. "I want you...to go for a drive with me."

She blinked repeatedly. "A drive?"

He exhaled in relief. "Yeah. A drive. Over the ridge. There's this place on Jonas's farm where you can look out over the valley. And sometimes, if the moon hangs right, you can see its reflection in the Upper Sunshine Reservoir. Wanna go?"

"Right now?"

"Why not? It's a gorgeous night."

Another bout of confusion manifested on Liv's face. "What about the rest of this wood?"

A slew of erection jokes he'd never be able to share bounced around in his head. "I'll finish tomorrow morning. Come on."

He grabbed the ax with one hand and swung it, burying its blade in the broad side of one of the logs. He then made quick work of his tailgate, cleaning it off and pushing back the cooler so he could close it. Together, they climbed in the truck and drove across the field to the east gate.

Brody opened and closed several gates before they reached their destination, all the while feeling Liv's thigh brushing against his as they bounced in the seat. The drive there was not a quick one, but it sure made for an adventure. Many times, Liv squealed in excitement and steadied her beer so it wouldn't spill when they bounded across ruts and bumps in the fields. He could admit to sometimes hitting them on purpose in order to throw her against him and hear her laughter. Her hand, braced on his thigh, wasn't bad either.

After pulling through and closing the last gate, he eased his truck along the pasture grass so as not to damage it. Sleepy steers, huddled in groups, stared at them as they passed by.

Liv sat up straighter and gazed out the rear window. "Oh my gosh, they're following us."

"That's because they think they're getting fed. They associate a pickup truck with buckets of grain."

Brody steered his Chevy along the fence and crested the hill. He threw it in park beneath a large oak and killed the engine. Liv swiveled in her seat, and her mouth gaped in awe at the view before her.

Like a page out of a vacation destination magazine, a breathtaking display of peaks and meadows, veiled with pines and firs, stretched for miles. A shimmering mirror of moonlit water lay tucked in a valley of hills. Beyond that rose the majestic Absaroka mountain range beneath a sea of twinkling stars in a midnight sky.

"Oh my gosh, Galven. This is amazing!"

She handed him her beer and inched to the edge of the seat. Her palm came down on his leg again as she pushed herself closer to the windshield. Any man with a working nervous system would stir at the feel of a woman's hand on his thigh. He was no different.

He doused the fire in his soul with a swig of her beer. *God, help me.*

"Brody, I can't believe how gorgeous this is."

"I know," he concurred, though his eyes weren't fixed on the scenery outside his truck. The view from the inside was a thousand times better.

Without tearing away her gaze, Liv leaned back and nestled herself against his chest. Brody hesitated but eventually threw an arm over her and pulled her close. The feel of her body pressed against his did little to ease the turbulence of his thoughts. From wondering if he reeked of perspiration to praying he'd have the strength to resist the urge of kissing her again, he couldn't relax.

"Brody?" she commenced.

He swallowed. "Yeah?"

"Do you ever stop and think where we'll be five years from now? Like if we'll still be doing the same old things we do now?"

He wasn't sure where she was going with this. "Meaning…"

"Meaning, if you'll still be working here and me at the Wagon Wheel." She reached over and took the beer from his hand, tipping it to her lips. "I don't want to be a waitress for the rest of my life."

Brody heard the despondence in her voice and manned up. "You know what I think?"

She rotated her head to meet his gaze. "What?"

He smoothed her hair away from her forehead and admired her rare beauty. He stroked the flawless skin on her face and even though her sweet, supple lips dared him to capture them in a kiss, it occurred to him that he might never get an opportunity kiss her ever again should she jet off to Nashville.

Ignoring every compulsion he had to do just that, he simply offered a smile. "I think that call you've been waiting for is gonna come in sooner than you think."

Liv sighed and sank back into his torso, her hand resting on his chest. "I don't know about that. I mean, I've been working hard to get a website up and running. And I have a Facebook page like my agent insisted. I've even recorded a few songs on YouTube to get some exposure while she supposedly works her magic with the record-label bigwigs. I just want this so bad, Galven, I can taste it."

Brody considered Liv's words and the earnest desire she had to see her dream come true. He respected how hard she worked to get her foot in the door and that she wasn't content to sit by and wait for something to happen. Whether it be by accident or by the connections of her agent, Olivia Langston was going to be a country music superstar. He knew it. As sure as eggs, he knew it.

Brody let his head fall back against the rear window and cast a glance outside his truck, staring at nothing in particular. The things she worried about were a far cry from what troubled him.

Liv thought of what she'd do if that call *never* came.

He worried about what he'd do when it did.

Just the thought of letting her go pierced his heart like a hard-driven horseshoe nail.

He closed his eyes and propelled those gloomy thoughts from his mind. Until the day when he'd have to say good-bye, he'd treasure every moment with her and be the man she needed him to be.

He glanced at Liv, all snuggled against his chest, and smiled. For now, what she needed from him seemed to be just a friend to lean on.

Chapter Six

"So, tell me what happened last week at the Wagon Wheel. I'm dying to hear it from the horse's mouth."

Olivia stopped strumming and splayed her fingers across the strings of her guitar, throwing her friend Regina a look from across the room. "What are you talking about?"

Regina plopped down beside her and reclined against the arm of the sofa. Her smile beamed as she crossed her arms. Her lips were perfectly lined in a shade of deep red, which, along with her soft brown hair and warm hazel eyes, accentuated her natural classic beauty. While Regina often remarked about needing to lose a few pounds, Olivia thought she was model perfect. "You know darn well what I'm talking about. The whole town's fussing about it."

"What, with Brody?"

"Yes, with Brody," Regina cried. "That whole thing about how he stuck up for you and tossed some wannabe cowboy around like a toy."

"Oh yeah. That." How could she forget? That was also the night she thought Brody confessed to wanting her, only to modify his words into something else. "What's there to tell? Some douchebag groped me, Brody got upset, and he bloodied the guy's nose."

Regina crossed her arms and smirked. "Aren't you forgetting the part where you told Jethro to take a hike?"

"I didn't tell Jethro to take a hike. I told him I was clocking out so I could make sure Brody was okay. He was pretty upset when he left."

"What else is new," Regina sneered.

"Don't do that," Olivia scolded.

"What?"

"Do what everybody else in this town does when it comes to Brody. He's not the screwup everyone makes him out to be."

"I know that. But, he *has* been in jail."

"Like, seven years ago, when he was a minor," Olivia defended. "How long is this town going to hold that against him?"

"If it's any consolation, I hold nothing against a man who comes to the aid of a woman," Regina said, suddenly endorsing him. "Especially a man who looks like Brody Galven." She fanned her face. "All those muscles and that teeny-weeny butt... I'd love to sink my teeth into it."

Olivia *wanted* to laugh when her friend growled and bit the air, but she wasn't in the mood to joke around about a guy who'd never be interested in her the way she was in him. It hurt too much.

"And don't get me started on his tatts," Regina ranted. "He looks like that lead singer from Maroon 5, except with lighter hair. And broader shoulders. Oh, I'm such a sucker for a bad boy."

While Regina raved on and on about Brody, Olivia spaced out on his long, muscular arms and the flamboyant sleeves that colored them. Inked with blue flames, pinup girls, and biomechanical paraphernalia, he resembled someone more from Orange County Choppers than Park County, Wyoming.

While his tatts lent him an air of distinction among the average residents of Meeteetse, it was the sleek muscle definition of his upper body she loved most. Having a job that revolved around tossing hay bales, roping steers, and splitting wood, it was no wonder the man had arms like a roughneck on an oil-drilling rig.

Thinking back to last week on the McKinley ranch, she could curl up in those arms every day of her life if Brody'd let her. Therein lay her problem. He might have been her best friend, but that was all she'd ever be to him.

"How do you do it, Olivia?"

Upon hearing her name, Olivia snapped out of her trance. "What?"

"I said, how do you keep your hands off him? I mean, best friends or not, I wouldn't be able to."

Olivia feigned a smile. "It's not because I haven't tried."

"Well, try a little harder, will ya? I know *I'll* never have a chance with the guy, so my best hope is through you."

Olivia pursed her lips and strummed a G chord. "Don't hold your breath."

Regina's exuberance faded as she regarded the bleakness on Olivia's face. Her hands came up to hide her openmouthed stare. "Oh, honey. Are you…"

"Am I what?"

"In love with him?"

Olivia tried to play it off as hogwash, but she'd never been a good liar. Regina reached for her hand and clasped it in hers. "And here I was going on and on about him like that. I had no idea."

"It's okay. It's not a big deal."

"Yes, it is," Regina contended. "Why didn't you tell me? Better yet, why haven't you told *him*? Don't you think he'd want to know?"

Now Olivia felt like laughing. "Yeah, right. So he can rip my heart out one more time? I don't think so."

"Are we talking about the same Brody Galven here? 'Cause if I recall, he can't seem to get enough of you. He's always protecting you, shoving his weight around at any other dude who tries to steal your affections. Hell, the man gets in a fight over you more often than bronc riders get bucked."

Olivia shook her head repeatedly. "Trust me, he may be a little overprotective, but it's not because he has feelings for me. I'm more like a sister to him."

Just as Olivia resumed plucking a tune, Regina clutched the neck of her guitar and arched a disbelieving brow. "Come again? A sister?" She narrowed her gaze. "Livie, I know you're an only child and you have no idea how siblings treat each other, but let me tell you this right now. Brody does *not* look at you like a sister."

"Then why did he backpedal out of a kiss so fast never to speak of it again? Or, better yet, why did he recant on a confession he made last week?"

"Wait, Brody kissed you? What else haven't you told me?"

Olivia squeezed her eyes shut and scratched her head. "It was a long time ago, Regina. Last year when I signed with my agent. I'd gotten off work, and after listening to my voice mails, I ran outside to tell Brody. I remembered being so excited that I leaped into his arms and popped a quick kiss on his lips. No big deal."

"No big deal?"

"Anyway... We both realized what had happened and...I remember the way he stared at me. The way he held me as he cupped my face. It was like he couldn't resist the pull of attraction any more than I could, and he surrendered." Olivia fell limp and smiled, staring off at a distance. "His lips were so soft, yet so domineering. And he smelled so good, like hay and leather and cologne."

"Yeah...go on."

Olivia straightened, and all reminiscent bliss disappeared. "That's it. He recoiled the second our tongues touched and hightailed it off the tailgate."

"And he never told you why?"

"Honestly, it was such an uncomfortable situation that I don't think either of us wanted to know why."

Regina waved her hand in front of her face as if she were erasing a chalkboard. "Okay so let's get back to his confession. Did he actually admit how he feels about you?"

Olivia shrugged. "Well...he said he wanted me. Then as soon as the words came out, he modified them."

"To what?"

Olivia huffed in frustration, loathing the fact that she had to relive this humiliating moment. She liked it better when Regina had no idea how she felt about Brody. "He changed it from 'I want you' to 'I want you...to take a drive with me.' Who does that?" she asked, lifting her arms in exasperation.

Regina tilted her head with an expression of sincere pity. "A man who's in love with you, but thinks he shouldn't be because it's not in your best interest. That's who."

Olivia pinched the bridge of her nose, trying to make sense of her friend's words. "Why wouldn't it be in my best interest if we dated?"

"I don't know. Maybe because the whole town still looks at him like he's a criminal...and he thinks you deserve better?"

"I couldn't care less what everybody thinks."

"That may be so, but a true gentleman always puts the welfare of others before himself. And I'd say Brody, given the respectful upbringing he had as a child, not to mention the ever-watchful brother who keeps him in line to this day, is the kind of man who'd put a lady first. Case in point, last week when he took on three guys single-handedly for you. Tell me I'm wrong."

Olivia pondered the scenarios in her head. She recalled the way Brody would watch her like a hawk and oftentimes come to her rescue, even when she didn't need him. He was always a gentleman when they hung out, and, in turn, he demanded it from others. She even remembered times when he'd act a little out of sorts the minute she got too close. What Regina said seemed conceivable enough, supporting the theory that he might have feelings for her, except for one thing. It didn't explain why at one moment he seemed so eager to kiss her, only to practically fall off the tailgate to get away from her in the next.

She'd seen the look on his face that day. He'd appeared confused. Surprised. Appalled. Not exactly the kind of reaction a girl wanted to see right after the start of an intimate, toe-curling kiss.

"You know," Regina intimated with a sly grin, "there's only one way to really know for sure how he feels about you, right?"

Olivia cringed, not quite ready to hear what that was. "And that is?"

Regina leaned in and whispered, "Ask him."

"No."

"What do you mean, no? He's your best friend. Surely you can talk with him about anything."

"Everything but the sappy crap. Galven's a rough and tough cowboy who likes his friend"—Olivia patted her chest, indicated herself—"to be as tough as he is. We fish. We ride horses. We drink beer. We don't sit around and discuss our feelings, Gina."

Regina reached for Olivia's hand and gave it a gentle squeeze. "Maybe it's time you did."

Olivia's cell phone danced across the coffee table. Inwardly, Olivia was grateful for the interruption and glanced at the display. "Oh my gosh!" She snatched up her cell and stared at it as it kept vibrating in her hand. "It's my agent!"

"Well, answer it!"

Olivia's heart kicked up in tempo. She wanted to scream with uncontrollable exhilaration. Was this the call she'd been waiting for all her life? Was this the day all her dreams would come true?

She jumped up and handed her guitar to her friend, gawking at the screen on her phone as if it were the president of the United States. She stepped over Regina's legs and paced the living room floor, shaking her hand vigorously. "Oh my gosh, I cannot believe this. What if—"

Regina sprang to her feet and landed in a soccer-goalie stance. "Would you just answer the damn thing!"

Olivia drew a huge breath and swiped the screen, then put it to her ear. "Hello?"

"Hello, Olivia, this is Sarah Saulita. I have good news for you. Do you have time to talk?"

She swallowed, trying to relieve the sudden dryness in her throat. *Is this really happening?* "Yes, I can talk."

"Great. Well, I guess the easiest way to say this is how do you feel about coming to Nashville and recording an album with Capitol Records?"

Chapter Seven

Brody took off his hat and wiped the sweat from his brow, squinting under the brilliant afternoon sun. Righting his Stetson on his head, he stared at his opponent, tied to the hitching post in front of the corral.

He was a dandy of a horse, all black with one white sock. At a little over fifteen hands, he stood aloof and motionless, save for the occasional swish of his tail. Despite his big brown eyes and calm disposition, akin to a seasoned ranch mount, this five-year-old gelding—named Psycho— was rumored to be a monstrosity when mounted.

Jonas McKinley had come by the horse on a dare. The story went that no one, not even the most skilled riders in Texas, could handle the bronc without being kicked or thrown. One such hapless individual ended up in the hospital with a broken nose, a dislocated hip, and a torn rotator.

Jonas, being a practiced rider himself, claimed he could get the horse on a trailer without injury to himself or the animal. The owner, nearly ready to put the rogue down, told Jonas if he could haul it, he could have it.

Fast-forward three weeks, and now it was Brody's job to curry out the kinks. If he was successful, Jonas had mentioned that he could keep the horse.

Rod said it was foolish, proclaiming that the feral beast wasn't worth getting hurt. But Brody never backed down from a challenge, especially when it meant proving his brother wrong.

He tightened the buckle on his chaps and walked over to the horse in a nonthreatening manner. The horse bowed its neck to see who approached and, after making eye contact with Brody, licked its lips.

Brody breathed easier. From Psycho's cues, Brody determined that the quarter horse had remembered him from yesterday's lesson, indicating that perhaps today's training might go a little smoother. He rewarded the horse with a good neck rub. In turn, Psycho nudged Brody's chest, enjoying the positive physical contact.

"All right, buddy," Brody soothed, scratching its muzzle. "All this week, we've worked on your trust level. Now let's see how you do with a saddle."

He led the horse into the corral, and for the next few hours, he worked at getting the gelding accustomed to the tack. Starting with the saddle pad, he rubbed it along the horse's body, against its flanks, and up its neck. He even took time tossing the pad over its back, all the while demonstrating that the horse had nothing to fear.

Next came the saddle.

Again, Brody allowed the horse all the time it needed to get acquainted with the strange-smelling item until he was able to ease it down over its back. The next hurdle was cinching it. Once that obstacle had been surmounted, he spent hours lunging the horse in a wide circle. The stirrups flopped and bounced against Psycho's ribs, causing the horse to spook at sporadic instances. With only a few minor crow hops to report, Brody thought it time to put some weight in the stirrups.

Psycho slowed his trot to a walk and then stopped in front of Brody. He stroked the animal, rewarding it for a job well done. However, the most challenging feat had yet to come. With a gentle but firm grip on the rein, Brody bowed the horse's neck toward its own left shoulder and stepped into the stirrup, slowly lifting his other foot off the ground. Time after time, he pulled himself up—suspending his weight off the side of the horse—and dropped back down. Increasingly, he did so with more vigor and less ginger maneuvering. Eventually, he was able to swing his leg over and mount the horse completely.

Brody exhaled, feeling full of pride for such an

achievement. Despite his brother's disapproval, he reveled in the feeling of sitting astride a twelve-hundred-pound animal once deemed too crazy to ride. He reached forward and patted the warm hide beneath Psycho's long black mane. "Thata boy. See? That's not so bad, is it?"

"Wow, I'm impressed."

Brody flicked only his gaze toward the corral gate, where Jonas stood with one boot on the rail. "It only took all week to get to this point. Now I'm trying to decide if I should press my luck and see if he'll walk on or call it quits for the night."

"Hell, you got him this far," Jonas pointed out. "I think he's too tired to give you too much trouble. Urge him forward. See what he does."

Brody clicked his tongue, and, with a gentle flick of the reins, Psycho stepped forward, then halted, unsure of the situation. Brody felt the horse quiver beneath him, but encouraged it onward. In a split second, Psycho lunged into a trot, his eyes wide. Brody reined sharply to the left, keeping the horse's feet moving. In this instance, he hoped to utilize the horse's thinking side of its brain instead of its reactive side. The last thing he wanted was for Psycho to commence to bucking and send him sailing into the fence rails.

"Stay with him, stay with him," he heard Jonas say

behind him. "You got this."

Brody steered the horse in the opposite direction, following the path of a loose circle until Psycho relented. As a reward, he gave the horse control of its head, and again Psycho bounded forward with a little hop. Brody repeated the cycle of corrective commands until he had the animal trotting smoothly without fail.

He looked at Jonas and saw him clench and pump his fist in praise. Brody could hardly believe it himself. With a little time and effort, he'd taken an ill-tempered nag no one would dare mount and shaped it into a valuable, worthwhile steed. With a little more training, Psycho had the potential to be a fine cutting horse.

His cutting horse.

He wondered if Jonas was serious about letting him keep Psycho. Hoping to find out, he slowed Psycho's pace and carefully dismounted. Leading him out of the corral, he met Jonas near the water trough.

"Did you really mean it when you said if I could ride Psycho, I could have him?"

Jonas patted the horse's shiny black coat and nodded. "Meant every word."

Brody smiled as he watched the horse drink. "Thank you, sir." When Jonas dismissed his gratitude, he added, "No, I mean it. For everything. You're the only one in this town who's really given me a second chance."

"Every decent man deserves that, Brody. But realize, once I stretch out my arm for you, it only takes one time to cut it off. You understand?"

"I do. You have my word I won't ever let you down."

Jonas clasped his shoulder with pride. "Glad to hear that. Now how about you untack this horse and put him in his dedicated stall. There's not much else to be done tonight except for the watering, if you wouldn't mind doing that for me. Rod already left for the day, and Ava and I are leaving to go out to dinner."

Brody didn't hear anything past dedicated stall. "I'm not sure I heard you right, boss. Shouldn't I turn Psycho out to pasture?"

"Personally, I think he'd be more comfortable in the barn." Jonas beamed so big, his dimples popped. "Go have a look."

"Psycho has his own stall now?"

"I know it sounds a little presumptuous on my part, but if anyone was going to be able to ride that horse, I knew it would be you. So, consider it a gift. Go on." He gestured with a nod of his head. "Check it out."

Brody didn't know what to say. He had a fluttery, empty feeling in his stomach that wouldn't go away. It all seemed too much. And what had he done to deserve it anyhow? Did Rod have something to do with this?

All these questions and more bounced around in his head as he led Psycho into the barn. He looked at each nameplate on every door as he passed, anxious to see Psycho's. All around him, horses nickered and snorted. They seemed as curious as he was excited, because the stalls in this part of the barn were saved for the most precious horses, the working ones used by Jonas, Ava, and their staff.

Finally, at the last door, Brody stopped. Riveted on an upscale wood sign was a shiny metal nameplate with "Psycho" engraved in fancy western script. On either side a five-pointed star inside a circle had been branded with the initials M, c, K, representing the logo of the McKinley ranch. And below all that, held the inscription, OWNER: Brody Galven.

He took off his hat and swiped his brow in disbelief. He leaned closer and read it again. "Would you look at that," he said, throwing his arm around Psycho's neck. "I guess this means it's official."

Eager to see Psycho standing in his very own stall, he slid open the heavy pine door and walked him in. The horse immediately lowered its head and smelled the fresh layer of shavings lining the floor. Knowing the horse might very well roll, Brody immediately lifted its head and removed the bridle. With a few more tugs, he released the cinch and slipped off the saddle. "There you go, buddy. How's that feel?" he asked, rubbing the horse's sweaty hide where the pad had sat. "Now you can roll if you want."

Like the old saying about leading a horse to water, Brody knew Psycho wouldn't roll until he was good and ready. As he finished attending to Psycho's needs, he heard the crunching of gravel from a vehicle outside the barn. Figuring it was Jonas and Ava leaving for dinner, he was glad to know he was by himself. This meant he didn't have to rush through anything or work up a sweat doing it. He had all night. Given tomorrow was Sunday, a day off for all the ranch staff, he flirted with the idea of driving out on the ridge. Hell, if the stars were out, he might even sleep in the bed of his truck.

With those plans in his brain, Brody removed his chaps and hung them in the tack room before climbing the ladder to the loft above. As he threw down a bale of hay for Psycho, he thought of all the things he'd like to do with his new horse. He couldn't wait for the day when they could ride out to the ridge together and watch the sun go down. In his mind, there was nothing better than the view from a saddle.

"Need some help?"

The familiar female voice took Brody by surprise, and

he lost his footing on the second-to-last rung of the ladder as he came down. He caught his fall, but his boot hit the ground quite ungracefully. He looked up, and his heart skipped.

Liv wore his favorite pair of jeans and a mint-green tank that showed off both the curves of her chest and the light color of her eyes. Her long hair and full breasts bounced with each step she took in her matching green Justin boots.

"Didn't mean to scare you, Galven," she said, almost laughing. "I thought you would've heard me pull up."

Brody dusted off his jeans, playing it cool. "I heard a vehicle, but I assumed it was Jonas and Ava."

She thumbed behind her and bit her lip. "Yeah, they were pulling out as I was pulling in. Do you think they mind that I'm here?"

"Nah, Jonas and Ava are cool." He ignored the thumping in his chest, finding it crazy that his heart beat faster with Liv than when he'd mounted Psycho for the first time. He carried the bale of hay over to his stall and flipped it over, knot side up, in front of the door. "Come here and look what Jonas did."

Liv walked up beside him and shoved her hands in her back pockets. "What a beautiful nameplate." Her eyes lit up. "Oh wow! Your name is on here too."

Brody grinned as he took out his pocketknife and cut the bale twine. "Pretty cool, huh?"

"Hell, yeah," she agreed, peeking through the wrought iron bars at the black horse inside. "Wait. Isn't Psycho that crazy horse that sent some poor guy to the hospital?"

Brody nodded an affirmative.

"That wild horse that no one's been able to break?" Liv inquired further.

"No one, until now," Brody declared proudly.

"Nah-uh," Liv said, crossing her arms. "You broke this horse?"

"Yes, ma'am." It sounded even better coming from Liv's mouth. He couldn't wait until word spread to his brother.

"What made you decide to do that, Galven?"

"Well," he began as he slid open the door and tossed the hay in the rack, "Jonas said if I broke the horse, I could keep him. So, I thought why not?" The stall door made a loud thud when he closed it, which emphasized the importance of what he'd succeeded in doing that no one else had.

"You could've gotten hurt."

Brody heard the concern in her voice and was glad. Glad to know someone cared enough about him to worry. Rod fretted over him all the time, but that was different.

His concern was over the family name and the hope that Brody wouldn't tarnish it.

He leaned against the stall door, crossing his arms and ankles. "But I didn't."

Liv threw a punch at his arm. "You're such a cocky bastard. It's no wonder trouble follows you wherever you go."

"Is that what you're calling yourself these days? Trouble?"

Liv made a face at his jest and turned on her boot heel. She dragged her hand along the bars of the stall as if she were strumming a harp and listened to the soft, muffled sound it made off her fingers. Brody sensed she was dithering but couldn't quite guess why. He busied himself by putting away the tack, brushes, and combs he used on Psycho, knowing full well she'd be the one to break before he did.

"You haven't asked me why I'm here yet," Liv hinted.

"On a hunch, I suppose it's 'cause you're bored and have nothing to do on a Saturday night."

"Close but no cigar." She bit her lip as she smiled, looking as if she were dying to spill the beans. "Try again."

Brody drew the hose from the reel and turned on the water, filling Psycho's bucket through the bars. "Let's see..." He thought of the last time he'd seen her and rummaged through those memories for an idea. One popped into his head, and he laughed. "Jethro fired you for walking out on your shift."

Liv chuckled with him. "No, he didn't fire me." She inched back toward him, her hands crossed behind her. "But I did quit."

He stiffened, not expecting that. "You quit? Why?"

Her smile beamed brighter than ever, which confused the shit out of him. Being jobless was not something to be happy about.

Liv took the last step forward in a hop and clapped her hands once. "My agent called last night. I'm going to Nashville."

Chapter Eight

Brody felt the ground slip from under him. He knew one day he'd hear those words come from her mouth, but not this soon. He wasn't ready. She hadn't given him time to prepare.

"Brody?" she said, touching his forearm. "Did you hear me? I'm going to Nashville."

Hearing it a second time didn't help matters. "Right. I heard you. Nashville."

"I cannot believe this is happening," she said, dancing on her tiptoes in elation.

He couldn't believe it either. The pain of having to say good-bye to her balled up like a stone in his throat. How was he going to survive without her? "H-how soon do you leave?"

"Tomorrow!" she exclaimed. "Oh my gosh, this is all too fast."

Damn right it is.

He heard the sound of spilling water and realized

Psycho's bucket was overflowing. "Shit." He swept past her and carried the hose to the next stall. Topping off another bucket, he tried to come to terms with Liv leaving Meeteetse. It mattered little how he felt about it. She was going to go regardless. She *needed* to go, because scoring a record label, recording music, and touring the country was her lifelong dream.

She needed to go, he reaffirmed. But he needed *her*.

"Galven?" she asked, circling him until she stood in front of him. "Aren't you going to say anything? Aren't you happy for me?"

"Of course, I'm happy for you." He no more believed his words than she did. He had to get ahold of himself and stop acting so selfish. This was her moment to shine. Her day to rejoice. He'd had his this afternoon with Psycho.

"Brody, seriously. What's wrong? Why are you not happy for me? This is big shit here. Capitol Records is offering me a record label. Do you understand that? Capitol Records!"

A horse neighed, and Brody broke eye contact with her. He glanced down at the bucket and proceeded to the next stall. Squeezing past her, he shoved the hose between the bars and into another bucket. He closed his eyes and drew a deep breath. *Be happy for her! At least fake it, for crap's sake!*

Liv marched up in front of him and planted her hands on her hips. "Seriously? This is how you react to my getting a once-in-a-lifetime deal?"

"I'm sorry. I'm a little overwhelmed right now. What do you want me to say?"

"Oh, I don't know, how about 'Liv, that's awesome!' Or how about 'Wow, you did it! Your hard work paid off! Knock the socks off Nashville, babe!' Anything! But no. You stand there and fill water buckets."

"The horses need water. It's important."

"More important than wishing me good luck? More important than rooting me on before I venture to some strange state to chase a dream at which I'm scared to death I'll fail? More important than saying good-bye to your best friend?" Liv's eyes welled, and a tear trailed down her cheek. As quick as it fell, she wiped it away. "I thought out of everyone in this town, you'd be the happiest for me. That you'd be the most supportive. That you'd be my…biggest fan. I guess I was wrong."

Brody's heart tore in two when he heard her voice crack. And he nearly died the minute she turned to walk away. He couldn't let her walk out believing he didn't care.

"Liv, wait!" he shouted, running to turn off the water. He caught up with her and stopped her short of exiting the barn. He grabbed her arms and stared into her red, tear-filled eyes. "I do care. I care…a lot about you."

She wiped her tears again, this time with aggravation. "Really?" She bounced her body on one hip. "You have a strange way of showing it."

He squeezed his eyes shut, at a loss for how to make her understand. "I know, I know. I'm not very good at this. It's just complicated. It's hard, Liv."

"Then let me make it easy for you, Galven." She pushed out of his grip and shot him a cold look that pierced his chest. "Good-bye."

Liv bypassed him again, and he panicked. "Liv, come back. Please, come back. Don't leave. Liv…Liv…Liv!"

She was almost to her car, and it happened.

"Dammit, Olivia Langston, I love you!"

She stopped. Her hand froze on the door handle. From where he stood, he could see her trembling. Was that anger? Was that shock? Was that stupid of him to say, on the night before she was leaving for Nashville? *Probably*.

He knew he should say something else. Something to get her to turn around and look at him, but he didn't have the confidence to do so. He feared if he said the wrong thing, she'd flip him the bird, hop in her car, and throw gravel speeding away.

He took off his hat with one hand and ran his other through his hair. Holding his Stetson over his heart, he gathered his bravado and drew in a breath. "Liv," he said, his voice straining from the dryness in his throat. "I love you. I have always loved you."

Still, she didn't move.

He clenched his fists and opened his heart a little more. "I know that hearing me say that may seem really strange, coming from your best friend. But I can't let you leave thinking I'll be fine once you're gone."

Nothing.

It killed him that she was but ten feet away and he couldn't see her face. He shuffled his feet, impatience setting in. "Liv, I can't take this anymore. Either turn around and face me, or get in your car and leave. But realize this. If you leave, no one will ever love you like I do. No one."

Slowly, Liv turned around. Her face was wet with tears as if she'd cried a river. He'd never seen her this upset. Without so much as a word, she walked toward him. Step by step, he stared at her, having no idea what to expect. Aside from seeing the pain written on her face, he didn't know if she was angry or saddened. With women, he heard it could go either way.

The closer she got to him, the faster she walked. From out of the tears burst a smile so beautiful, he almost thought he imagined it. At arm's length, she leapt into his, blessing him with a kiss hot enough to set the barn on fire.

Brody held her tight, relishing this moment as if it were his last hour on earth. She smelled of strawberries and tasted like cinnamon and salt. Her tears mixed with whatever gum she chewed on the way there made this kiss all the more memorable, because this would be a day he'd never forget.

Her hands came up to his face, and she pulled away, staring into his eyes. "Please tell me I'm not dreaming."

Brody touched his forehead to hers. "You're not, Liv. You're not."

Brody dipped his head and captured her lips, kissing her like a soldier going off to war. His hands threaded in her hair and then down her back, squeezing her body against the hard plane of his chest muscles. She arched against him, surprised when a tiny mew escaped her. He groaned and devoured it, kissing her deeper. His tongue pierced her lips and swept through her mouth, igniting a fire so intense, she wanted to scream.

Brody's arms tightened around her, and he carried her toward his truck. He opened the passenger door, tossed his cowboy hat on the dash, and flopped her down on the seat.

Climbing in after her, he unbuttoned his shirt and

peeled it away from his shoulders. His biceps bulged beneath a colorful canvas of tattoos, and a dark layer of soft beard complimented his high, chiseled cheekbones. His blue eyes darkened with desire, while his close-cropped brown hair added an edgy look to his handsome face. He was the quintessential bad boy Olivia knew she shouldn't fall for, but here she was, diving deep.

He crawled across her body and hovered, smiling just a little. Brody didn't often show happiness, as he was more the pensive, brooding type. But for once, she saw a hint of mischievousness in his expression, a playful appeal to his rugged side.

In all the years she'd known him, she couldn't remember when he'd looked as roguishly sexy as he did now. Perhaps it was because he lingered above her without a shirt on. Or maybe because he no longer hid how he felt about her.

"Do you know how long I've waited for this, Liv?"

Did he know how long *she* had?

She'd been dreaming of him for longer than she could remember, and until he'd kissed her so passionately, she wouldn't have believed he felt the same. Who would've thought after all these years of being friends that she and Brody were about to cross into something so extraordinary. Something so much more than just a platonic relationship.

The anticipation of Brody's intimate touch sent a thrill through her whole body.

"Then let's not wait another second more," she whispered and pulled his heavy body down upon hers.

Chapter Nine

Brody couldn't stop smiling as he drove down a two-lane back road that led toward the Langston residence. Liv sat in the passenger seat of his truck, flushed and dreamily gazing out the windshield while he rested his elbow on the open window. The cool night air blew in as he relived the heated moments he had spent with Liv.

After a few miles of silence, she finally broke his reverie with a question.

"Now that we've done this, Brody, do you have any regrets?"

He pondered her words carefully. "Just one," he admitted. "I regret I didn't have the guts to tell you how I felt sooner. I would've liked to have had more time with you before you jet off to Nashville." He expected some sort of reply from her, but when she didn't, he regarded her closely. "You're still going to Nashville tomorrow, right?"

"I don't know." She shrugged.

"What do you mean you don't know?"

"I mean, things have changed now. There's more to consider—"

Brody hammered down on the brakes and pulled over to the side of the road. He threw the shifter in park and whirled in the seat to face her. "There's nothing to consider. You're going to Nashville, Liv, and that's that."

Her jaw clenched and she cast him a stern look. "Don't you think that's *my* decision?"

"Dammit, Liv. I knew I shouldn't have told you how I felt. I should've kept my damn mouth shut."

"What is that supposed to mean, Galven?"

"It means I don't want you throwing away your dreams over me. I'm not worth it."

"Who says I'm throwing them away?"

"You will be if you don't get on that plane tomorrow."

Liv furrowed her forehead in confusion. "Why are you so adamant about me leaving?"

He closed his eyes, finding it hard to look at her. She was so beautiful and desirable that anything she asked for, he'd give her. Even the moon if he could.

"Brody, if I do this, there's no telling how soon I'll get to come home. It could be weeks, months from now. I don't know." She reached out and laid her hand over his. He ignored the temptation of her touch, the allure of her voice when she pleaded her case. "I've wanted you for so long…and now that I have you…I'm not sure I'm ready to give you up."

Brody clenched his teeth. He had to remain strong. "If you don't get on that plane, there is no us."

Her hand slid from his. "What are you saying?"

He opened his eyes and riveted her with an intense stare. "If you throw away your only chance at stardom for me, I'll never forgive myself. What kind of man would I be if I held you back? How could you continue to love and respect me if I didn't push you to chase your dream?" He edged closer and cradled her face, catching her tears in his palms. "It kills me to tell you to leave. Especially when I'm finally holding the one person in my life I can't live without." He brushed his thumb across her cheek and softened his voice. "But because you are the only thing that is right in my world…I *must* do right by you. You deserve nothing less." He drew in a breath, holding back his own emotions. "Now, you're going to get on that plane…and you're going to knock the socks off Nashville. You hear me?"

Through their tears, they shared a laugh recalling her words from earlier this evening. He pressed his forehead against hers, and swallowed the lump in his throat. "Tell me you're going to Nashville, Liv."

She nodded.

"I need to hear you say it, baby."

"I will," she whispered. "I will go to Nashville. And I will make you so proud of me."

He looked deep in her eyes, brushing back a flyaway strand of hair from her face. "You already do."

****

After more than a four-hour trip through Wyoming the following evening, Brody parked his truck in the lot across from the ticketing entrance of the Jackson Hole Airport and rounded the vehicle to open Liv's door. He took in the majestic snow-capped Teton mountain range standing at an impressive thirteen thousand plus feet, less than a few miles away. For once in his life, he felt small. Unimportant. He wondered if this was how all the significant others of famous people felt.

Holding her door open, he took her by the hand and helped her out of the seat. The wind blew her hair in whips of wild ebony. He reckoned she was thankful she hadn't worn that sundress he liked so much.

"Are you ready?" he asked, though he felt more inclined to ask himself the same question.

Liv peered out toward the mountains and watched a plane come in for a landing. "I guess so." She bit her nail and tilted her head up to look at him. "Not really."

"You'll be fine," he tried to soothe.

"I've never flown before, Galven."

He smiled at his rough and tough tomboy falling apart. He lifted her suitcase from the bed of the truck and grabbed her guitar case from the seat. "I've not either, but I heard the takeoffs and landings are the hardest to get through. Close your eyes and think of me. I'll have my arms around you the whole time."

"I wish you were coming with me."

Brody nodded, determined not to make this harder than it already was. "Call me when you land. And when you find your agent at the terminal. And when you get to your hotel. And before you go to sleep tonight."

Liv giggled at his overprotectiveness, though he was serious.

He walked her to the beautiful lodge-like building and stopped at the glass doors at the front entrance. He set her guitar and suitcase on the sidewalk. "Are you sure you're going to be able to maneuver all this on your own? What the heck did you pack?"

"Some necessities."

He pulled her into his arms and hugged her tight. "Okay, so your mother knows your flight schedule, right? I don't have to call her?"

Liv swung her upper body outward, giving him that puppy dog look. "It wouldn't hurt if you did. In fact, it might make her feel better to know you cared enough to call her."

June, Liv's mom, was a hard-nosed, hard-working female who didn't seem to notice the good in any man, especially since both her father and husband had abandoned her. Though Brody had always tried to be courteous toward the bitter woman, he knew one phone call was not about to change fifty years of intense animosity. "She doesn't like me much. I can tell."

"Mama likes you," Liv insisted. "She's just protective of me. Surely you, of all people, can understand that."

Precious time with Liv was running out, and he didn't want to spend it debating June's hang-ups. He cupped the back of Liv's head and pulled her against his chest. "Yeah, yeah. I hear you."

"Thanks, Galven. Oh, and tell Rod thanks for helping you get my car back home. I was so out of it last night, I completely forgot about leaving it at Jonas's after we… you know."

"Not a problem."

"And speaking of Jonas, tell him I'm sorry that I kept you from splitting the rest of that wood."

"I think he'll understand."

"Oh, and one other thing! Will you—"

Brody seized her face and pulled her into a kiss to get her to shut up. It worked like a charm. Even better, he was able to savor the taste of her one last time before she said good-bye. He knew letting her get on that plane was going to be difficult, but he never expected it to be this hard. Next to burying his father, this was definitely the toughest thing he'd ever had to endure.

"What are you going to do while I'm gone?" she asked as he slowly pulled out of the kiss.

He gave it some thought. "Might school Psycho some more, turn him into a cutting horse. Thought about painting Mom's porch for her. She'd like that, I think. Maybe see if Mr. Corinth still has that old 1953 Chevy 3100 he wants to fix up. Aside from those things, I'll be sitting around missing you. But don't worry. No matter how long you're gone, I'll still be here, waiting for you."

Liv picked up her guitar case with one hand and grabbed her heavy suitcase with the other. Brody opened the door for her, but she hesitated to go through, rocking him with a smile that beat all. "I love you, Galven."

With his heart in his throat, he lunged forward and wrapped his arms around her, crushing her lips in another searing kiss. He memorized her scent, her curves beneath his hands, and her sweet whimper in his ears. "I will always love you, my dear sweet Liv."

He tipped his hat and backed away toward his truck, unable to tear his gaze from her. She broke first, which he figured she would, as she had a plane to catch. But little did she know, he'd stay in his vehicle for the next two hours until he personally saw her plane take off, all the while longing for his Liv to come back home.

THE END

AUTHOR'S NOTE

If you enjoyed *Longing for Langston*, and are dying to find out how Brody gets along with Liv jumpstarting her career in Nashville, then I encourage you to read the continuing books in this series to find out.

For your reading enjoyment, I've included a segment from the next book in the series, *Made for McKinley*. Just turn the page.

*All are meant to be stand-alones (and can be read in any order), but for a more satisfying "happily ever after," reading in order is helpful and encouraged.

****

Take a trip out West and meet Brody, Jonas, and Cole—the three sexy, rugged cowboys who rope and run the McKinley ranch, as well as the women who try to tame them.

MAVERICKS OF MEETEETSE
A cowboy romance series set in the small town of Meeteetse, Wyoming.

Longing For Langston, Novella Book 1
Made for McKinley, Book 2
Falling for Forester, Book 3

Sincerely,
Renee

made for

mckinley

jonas & ava

book 2

Chapter One

Ava Wallace watched the rugged cowboy dismount from his horse after a long day's work mending fence. A blue-and-white plaid shirt covered long, muscular arms. Short blond hair peeked out from beneath his white straw Stetson, while dark blond stubble shadowed his jaw. He had eyes as blue as denim and lashes as black as coal, a striking contrast to the lighter brows dusting his chiseled face. He came from Irish descent, at least on his father's side, but Ava swore he had a bit of Norse in him too.

Clad in tight jeans and weathered chaps, he led his faithful steed toward the east pasture gate. Dust wafted at his heels, and his handsome face glistened with perspiration under the Wyoming summer sun.

She had offered to go with him, but he was a stubborn man. From the many years working this five-thousand-acre ranch, she'd learned not to fight a losing battle. Men like him did not bend easily, nor did they back down at the first sign of trouble. Two hundred head of cattle threatening to roam free because of a broken fence was not necessarily an ordeal but something that came with the territory of being a modern-day cowboy.

Reckoning her chores could wait, Ava smiled as she continued to watch him from inside the barn. He might not have known it, but she enjoyed gazing at him. Everything he did was remarkable. Whether he tossed a bale of hay, roped a running steer, or simply leaned against a fence, he was worth watching.

She made herself more comfortable against the nearest barn post, while the spent cowboy made haste to cool himself at the water trough. She knew the ritual. First came the leather gloves.

He'd tug them off, then stuff them in his back pocket. After that, he'd remove his cowboy hat and swipe his brow with his sleeve. Replacing the Stetson atop his head, he'd lean against the blackboard fence and patiently wait as his horse, Winchester, drank.

As a man of habit, he did it all without fail.

Finally, Winchester lifted his head and shook his body. Dirt and grit clouded around both of them, but neither seemed to mind. In fact, the man praised his horse with a good pat on the neck. That gesture alone was one of the things she loved about him. He might have been a rough and tough cowboy on the outside, but inside he had an unashamed gentleness for the animals under his care.

Ava recalled the saying: *You can always tell how a man*

treats his woman by the way he treats his horse. She sighed and went back to mucking the horse stalls, reminiscing how she used to be on the receiving end of that cowboy's consideration—when he couldn't keep his hands off her. When he'd back her into a stall and kiss the daylights out of her every chance he got.

She missed those days.

When they'd first met seven years ago, nothing seemed to get in the way of their passionate, almost volatile relationship—not even his high-dollar working cattle ranch and all the responsibilities that came with it. Sure, the ranch had also grown into a booming horseback riding facility, thanks to Ava's previous trick riding skills on the rodeo circuit, but she never expected things to fizzle out between them.

Her cowboy Casanova went by the name of Jonas McKinley, known far and wide as the best cattle rancher in all of Wyoming. But to Ava, he was the reckless young stud who stole her heart.

Some say she stole his, as he was never the type to settle down. She and Jonas entertained a ten-year age difference, which helped her gain the dreaded *Colorado Cougar* title she'd heard going around the small town of Meeteetse from time to time. If anyone had done any thieving, it was the dashing, blue-eyed, hard-nosed heartthrob armed with the most perfect butt east of the Rockies.

Ava grinned at the thought of the first time she'd taken a long gander at Jonas McKinley's tight tush…

****

Seven years before present day

It was the week before the annual Cheyenne Frontier Days. At age thirty-three, it wasn't the first time Ava had entertained thousands of fans with her daredevil saddle stunts. But it was the first time her horse had come up lame.

As she stood in the stall, soaking Ranger's hoof in a bucket of warm water and Epsom salts, she heard the solid footsteps of a man. She looked up from under the brim of her hat and noticed a young, sexy cowboy strolling toward her. He looked like one of the many contestants who was there to win big money and fame, but she'd found out earlier that he was the contractor who provided the steers for all the events. It was quite an accomplishment for a man his age to obtain, and she could admit to being impressed.

But that was as far as her admiration carried her.

Though she'd seen him many times that week among

the chaos of preparations, she always avoided drawing his attention. Her Achilles' heel had been the obvious age difference between them. She had a teenage son who was closer to his age than her own, and she thought it downright immoral to take an interest in him.

Ducking her head to avoid any such eye contact, Ava returned to the task of tending her horse's hoof. Even if he did notice her, she never imagined a handsome, eligible twenty-something cowboy would give a woman with deepening crow's feet the time of day. She thought he'd walk right by her.

A whistle broke the silence and then his voice. "Now, that's a nasty abscess."

Ava nearly jumped out of her jeans, dropping Ranger's hoof in the bucket. Water splashed her face, but her horse barely flinched and continued to munch on the hay hanging from a canvas bag in the corner. She clutched her chest and blew out a heavy breath. "Jesus, you startled me!"

"My bad." He sported a beautiful smile as he held out his hand. "And the name's Jonas, not Jesus."

Ava smiled back as she wiped the water droplets from her face, reluctant to make physical contact with him. Eventually, she shook his hand because she liked his sense of humor. "Jonas McKinley, right?"

"That's right."

Ava felt her hand tremble and jerked it away before he could notice.

Calm down, Ava. It's not like he's George Strait or something.

"Sorry if I scared you," he said, glancing at the way she fiddled with her shirt. "I didn't think you trick riders balked at anything."

Ava cleared her throat, surprised that he knew her profession. What surprised her more was how his simple touch did crazy things to her. Things she hadn't felt in a long time. Things that felt completely inappropriate right now.

Remember, Ava. He's just a man. Nothing special.

She forced her brain to articulate a blasé version of the guy. Dwelling on everything else that came to mind darn near killed her. She smiled. "You must have us confused with the bull riders. They're the fearless ones."

"I don't know. I think slinging your body upside down on a sprinting horse requires its own set of balls." He grinned and winked. "Pardon my French."

Ava laughed at his apology, though she'd heard worse things come from the mouths of bronc riders. "Well, for the record, I've never had a set of balls. So, I guess my excuse for riding beneath the belly of a horse is just plain idiocy."

He crossed his arms, then his ankles, and leaned

against the stall gate. "Skillful bravery maybe. But not idiocy."

"Call it what you want, Mr. McKinley, but it doesn't look like I'll be displaying either this time around." She sighed and glanced at her horse standing in a bucket. "I think the farrier quicked him."

"That's a damn shame."

She patted her horse and nodded. "I know. The farrier's a good friend of my late father, so this is not going to be an easy conversation to have with him."

"Late father, huh? I lost mine too. I'm sorry to hear about that."

"No, it's okay. It was a long time ago. Really."

"Well, it's still a damn shame. A shame I won't get to see you in spandex. Especially that black-and-silver one I saw you practicing in the other day. I think it's my favorite."

Ava felt her face flush. She could hardly look at him.

Did he really like the look of her body poured into that slick black-and-silver outfit or just all females in general who trick rode? At his age, she assumed the latter and reminded herself not to get her hopes up. The chances of him finding her even remotely sexy were slim to none. She chewed on her lip.

"My apologies if I came off too forward, ma'am."

Ava cringed at the sound of the sweet Southern drawl punctuating his confession. It wasn't the way he said it, but the title with which he chose to address her.

Ma'am.

Ugh! Ma'am is for proper older ladies. She was neither proper, nor old—at least she didn't feel old. Mature, maybe, but not old.

"What's with the face?" He leaned over the stall gate, and the cords in his neck tightened. Her gaze drew past the collar of his plaid Western shirt onto what she imagined to be warm, smooth skin. "Did I say something wrong?"

Her eyes met his, and she turned to mush. Looking into his crystalline eyes made her heart yearn for the tenderness of a man's sympathetic gaze. It had been a long time since she'd looked into the eyes of a handsome man. Far too long…

Ava quickly glanced away and shook off her ridiculous emotions.

Buck up, Ava. Don't let this green cowboy fluster you.

She straightened her back and stood her ground. No tantalizing tadpole was going to refer to her as old. "I'd rather you not call me ma'am."

He drew back and furrowed his brow. A cocky little smirk inched up the corner of his mouth as if he enjoyed her sudden feistiness. "My mama always taught me to be polite when talking to a woman, no matter how bad I wanna kiss her. So until you tell me what your name is, I'll be forced to continually unsettle you." He leaned closer. "And just so we're clear, I'd rather say things to arouse you."

Ava wasn't prepared for that comeback and could barely get past *"how bad I wanna kiss her."* Was he serious?

She shoved her hands in the pockets of her jeans so he wouldn't see her shaking.

"Ma'am?" he prompted. "Your name?"

Ava blinked repeatedly and forced herself back to reality. She looked at Jonas slouching with his elbows resting on the gate, his hands folded. The unabashed confidence he portrayed in his casual posture was more than she could handle. Younger or not, he was clearly more experienced in flirtatious dialogue.

"I'm sorry. My name is Ava. Ava Wallace."

He stood up straight and tipped his hat, his smile as broad as an arena barn. "Pleasure to meet you, Ava. Now, since I already struck a chord with you, I reckon I'll strike another."

"Excuse me?"

"Your horse. You seem pretty partial toward him, and I get that. If you're in need of a backup for the show this week, you're welcome to use mine. In his prime, he was a trick mount, but I bought and trained him to be a cutting horse. It's been about five years since he's galloped in a pen, but he's as sound as they come. He'll run like mad till you tell him to stop. Bomb goes off? Won't flinch a muscle. Dead broke."

He stroked the stubble on his jaw, and her attention zeroed in on his large hand. Ava imagined he probably knew a thing or two about how to properly use those strong, beautiful hands on a woman and how she'd give anything to be *that* woman.

"Obviously, you'll want to test him and see how he does running the pattern, but I'm thinking he'll have you saying 'hell yeah.'"

Ava dismissed the thoughts of his roaming hands and pretended to be indifferent. "That's a mighty nice offer, Mr. McKinley."

"Call me Jonas," he corrected. "Like you, I don't care to be called by stiff-collar titles."

"Okay."

"If you decide to take me up on my offer," he explained, pointing toward the corrals lining the rodeo grounds, "I'll be right over there."

Ava glanced in the direction he pointed. "Got it."

Jonas tipped his hat once more and strolled away, leaving her to ponder. And stare...

She took in his view from behind and nearly drooled. *It should be illegal for a man to have a butt like that.*

"Wooo, doggy, I agree. That fine butt *should* be illegal."

Ava whirled at the sound of a voice behind her. Her friend and fellow barrel racer, Crystal—or as she insisted, Crys, because the other was just too feminine—stood on the other side of the stall, her chin resting on the tops of her hands. Unlike Ava, Crys made no attempt to hide her gawking.

Ava covered her mouth in horror. "Did I seriously say those words out loud?"

"Yes, ma'am, you did." Crystal quickly looked in her direction and amended her statement. "I mean, Ava."

Ava rolled her eyes. "How long have you been eavesdropping?"

"Long enough to know his mama taught him right and he's dying to kiss you." Crystal giggled. "Or arouse you."

Ava shook her head and bent to check on Ranger's hoof. "Obviously, your mama never taught *you* right."

"Ah, now don't get your knickers in a bunch. I'm not gonna tell anyone that you got the hots for Mr. Sweet Tush over there. And you do, so don't deny it."

When it came to Crys, nothing slid past her. She came from a long line of bull riders, which meant she took no bull from anybody. A lie to her was as easily detected as a skunk in roses. Ava also knew the woman had loyalty, given they'd traveled the rodeo circuits together for over eleven years.

She recalled on one occasion how Crys had punched some cocky bull rider square in the nose for a degrading comment he made toward a young newbie barrel racer. He thought he was a big shot in front of his friends. Crys thought he needed to be put in his place.

Ava almost laughed, remembering how he'd mounted a longhorn steer the next day wearing a face-guard helmet. While it wasn't uncommon for a bull rider to protect his face from fracture in a competition, this guy never did—until that day. Irony was often a gifted comedian.

"So, what are you gonna do about McKinley's offer?" Crys asked as she spread shavings in her stall.

Ava lifted Ranger's leg and pulled the bucket away, ready to salve and Vetrap bandage the hoof. "I don't know. It sounds pretty dangerous to me."

"Are you talking about the man's horse or his kiss?"

Ava contemplated the question. "Both, I reckon."

Crys threw down the last of the shavings with a very devious grin. "I can't speak for borrowing another man's horse, but I don't think a kiss ever killed anyone."

MADE FOR McKINLEY
Mavericks of Meeteetse, Book 2 (Jonas & Ava)

Former trick rider Ava Wallace works the five-thousand-acre McKinley ranch and loves the man who owns it. Only trouble is, they've been living together for over seven years, and she can't help but think things have changed between them. Her rough-and-tough cowboy used to be relentless with his affection, unable to keep his hands off her. Now, he barely has the time.

Cowboy cattle rancher Jonas McKinley can't seem to catch a break. Between his hardworking live-in girlfriend feeling like they don't connect and the nuisance grizzly that keeps tormenting his livestock, he must overcome the troublesome challenges that threaten his lucrative family farm before he loses what he's worked so hard to keep. Faced with a difficult choice, Jonas has to decide what matters most: Ava or his ranch.

FALLING FOR FORESTER
Mavericks of Meeteetse, Book 3 (Cole & Crys)

Cowboy cattle rancher Cole Forester likes things the way they are—quiet, no-frills, and uncomplicated. He's a glorified bachelor with only a dog as his companion, totally content to live a solitary life next to the McKinley ranch. That is until a cute little barrel racer shows up looking for a job as a ranch hand.

Tomboy Crys Willingham hangs up her rodeo hat and heads to where her friend Ava Wallace lives, hoping to score a job that doesn't involve the risk of broken bones every time she mounts up. But once she lays eyes on Cole, it seems it's her vulnerable heart that's in danger of breaking.

ABOUT THE AUTHOR

RENEE VINCENT is a *USA Today* bestselling author of romance and women's fiction. Her books have earned numerous accolades, including a #1 Bestseller for Viking Romance.

She lives on a secluded hundred-acre horse farm in the rolling hills of Kentucky with her husband, two beautiful daughters, and a few fur babies who've managed to weasel their way into a couple of books.

When she's not writing, she loves to decorate (and redecorate) her home, knit cozy blankets, send homemade cards to family and friends, and concoct her own versions of recipes to pass down to her girls.

www.ReneeVincent.com

Books By Series

Vikings of Honor Series
Sunset Fire, Book 1
Emerald Glory, Book 2
Souls Reborn, Book 3
Tempered Steel, Book 4

Mavericks of Meeteetse Series
Longing for Langston, Brody & Liv, Book 1
Made for McKinley, Jonas & Ava, Book 2
Falling For Forester, Cole & Crys, Book 3

Jamett & Joseph Series
The Start of Something Good, Book 1
The Road to Something Better, Book 2
The Gift of Something Grand, Book 3
Something's Bound to Happen, Books 1 - 3

Stand Alone Novel
Silent Partner

If you enjoyed this book by Renee Vincent, please consider leaving an honest review at your favorite vendor. Reviews not only give credibility to an author's work, they also help other readers find quality books worth reading.

ReneeVincent.com